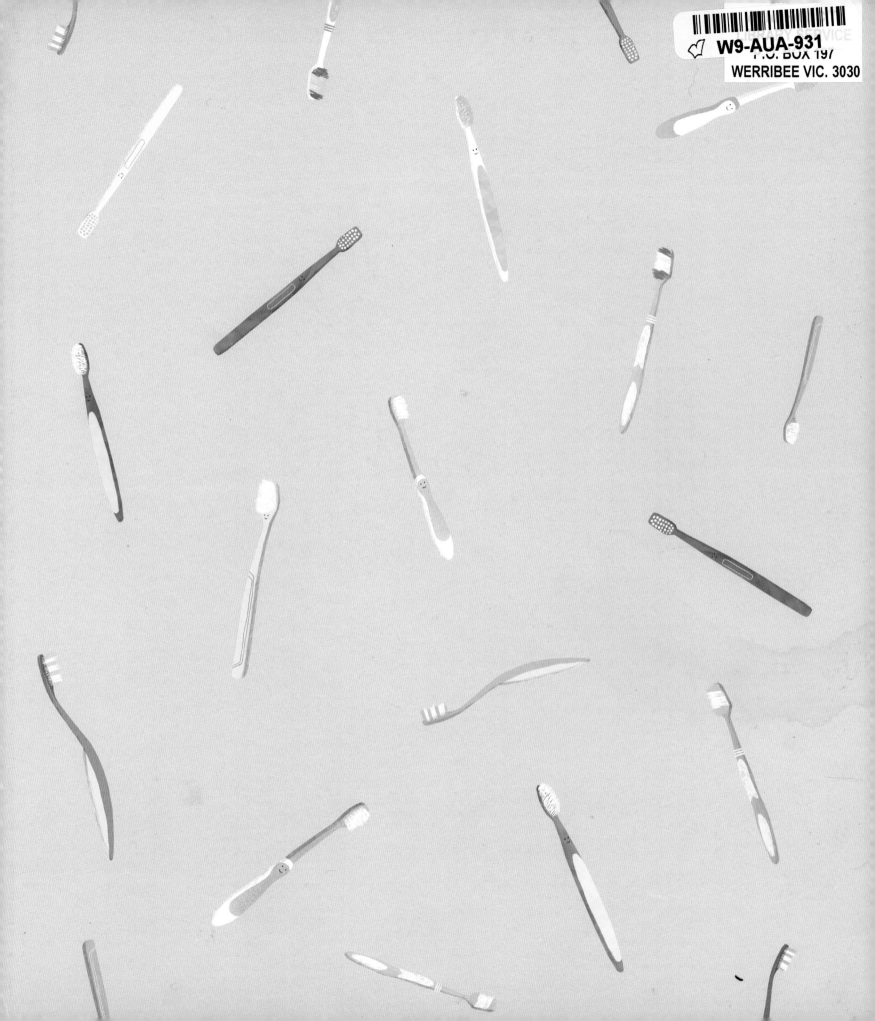

For my mummy, Jane Sparling,
and every child she's ever taught – M.G.L.

For Florence and everyone who is trying to reduce
their use of single-use plastics – D.R.

First published 2020 by Walker Books Ltd
87 Vauxhall Walk, London SE11 5HJ
2 4 6 8 10 9 7 5 3 1
Text © 2020 MG Leonard Ltd. Illustrations © 2020 Daniel Rieley Cover lettering Letters by Julia
The right of M.G. Leonard and Daniel Rieley to be identified as author and illustrator respectively of this
work has been asserted by them in accordance with the Copyright, Designs and Patents Act 1988
This book has been typeset in Adamina
Printed in China

British Library Cataloguing in Publication Data: a catalogue record for this book
is available from the British Library

ISBN 978-1-4063-8969-2 (Hardback)
ISBN 978-1-4063-9181-7 (Paperback)

www.walker.co.uk

WALKER BOOKS
AND SUBSIDIARIES
LONDON • BOSTON • SYDNEY • AUCKLAND

THE TALE OF A TOOTHBRUSH

M.G. LEONARD   Illustrated by DANIEL RIELEY

Six-year-old Sofia was allowed to choose her own toothbrush. She picked one as yellow as sunshine and drew an S on its tummy.

"Now everyone knows this is my toothbrush," she said.
"His name is Sammy."

Sofia cleaned her teeth with Sammy every morning before school

and every night before bed.

Sammy was a very happy toothbrush.

One day Sofia's mum saw that Sammy's bristles were worn out.
"Oh dear!" she said. "Sofia needs a new toothbrush."

And she
threw
Sammy
away.

"That's not Sammy," cried Sofia, when she saw a red toothbrush beside the sink. "Where is he?"

But the dustmen had emptied the bins and taken Sammy away.

It was dark inside the black rubbish sack.
Sammy was squashed up against an empty
shampoo bottle.

"Hello," he said. "I'm Sofia's toothbrush."

"Not any more you're not," said the grumpy shampoo bottle.
"You're rubbish now."

"We're doomed," wailed a plastic bag, "and I only got used once!"

I want Sofia, Sammy thought. I don't like it in here.

The blast of a ship's horn
startled Sammy.

"What's happening?" he squeaked.

"We're on a boat," said a crushed
soap box.

"You mean, I'm a sailor?" Sammy
smiled. "Wait till I tell Sofia."

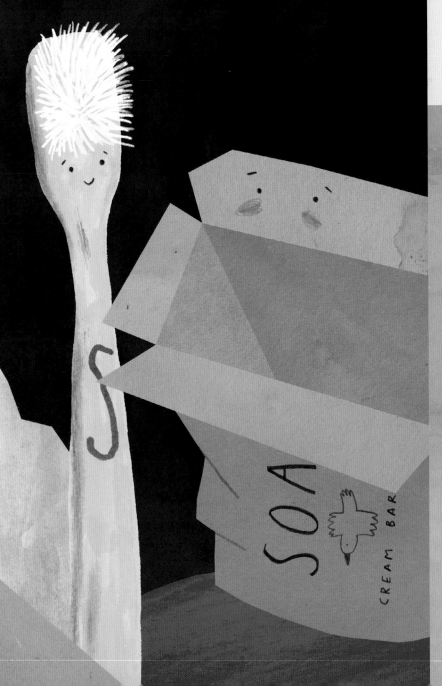

Sammy sailed across
the sea for countless days
and nights.

Then there was a grinding
sound and a clang, followed
by a dazzling light.

Sammy was tipped up, and
tumbled down with jars, bottles,
wrappers and bags.

This new, hot place was a long way from Sofia.
A big rat scampered up and sniffed him.
"Help me, please," Sammy said. "I sailed here on
a boat, but I want to go back home."

"Hold tight." The rat took Sammy between his teeth and
dragged him to the river. "This river leads to the sea.
Go back the way you came. Good luck."

"Thank you, friend rat,"
Sammy called, as he floated away.

The sun rose and the sun set a hundred times,
as Sammy sailed the seas.

He washed up on a golden beach and saw a pink
toothbrush dancing with a plastic bottle under a palm tree.

"Where am I?" he asked them.

"The Island of Love," replied the pink toothbrush.

"Our love will last as long as we do," said the
plastic bottle, embracing the toothbrush.

"For ever."

"I can't stay," Sammy said, as a wave
tugged at his toes. "I'm searching for
the way home to Sofia."
"Does she love you?" the pink toothbrush asked.
"Oh yes. She drew an S on my tummy."
"Then you must find her," the plastic bottle cried.

Sammy sailed for days and weeks and months, swirling and whirling in the middle of the ocean.

He met a detergent bottle who thought it was a pirate ship, tried to talk to a deflated balloon,

and swam up to a raft of plastic straws who had banded together. None of them could help him find his way home.

Sammy began to give up hope.

"Dearest star," he said, as he bobbed about in the ocean,

"I'm lost. Can you help me find the way back to Sofia?"

"Go north by north east," said the first star.

"Twinkle, twinkle," said the second.

In the morning an albatross flew down, landing on
the water beside Sammy.

"Yum!" The albatross pecked his tummy.

"Ow! Don't eat me," Sammy cried.

"I'm plastic. I'll make you sick."

"But I'm hungry," the albatross squawked.

"Then eat a fish," Sammy replied.

"Aren't you a fish?" the albatross asked, cocking his head.

"I'm a toothbrush," Sammy told him,

"trying to get home."

ORANGE
JUICE

CRUNCH

"Where is home?" asked the albatross.

"The stars told me to sail north by north east,"
 Sammy replied.

"I bring luck to those who sail the seas."
 The albatross blinked.

"I will help you."

He dipped his head and scooped the
yellow toothbrush up in his beak.
"I'm flying!" Sammy whooped, as he rose up towards
the clouds. "If only Sofia could see me now."

The albatross flew over oceans and high mountain ranges until, at last, they reached Sofia's house. He placed Sammy on the doormat and whispered goodbye.

"LOOK! Mummy, it's Sammy!" Sofia hugged the yellow toothbrush.

"It can't be," her mother frowned.

"It is, you can see where I drew the S."

"But you CANNOT clean your teeth with him Sofia," her mother said. "He's dirty."

Sammy's heart sank.

Sofia stared at the old yellow toothbrush.

"I may not be able to brush my teeth with him," she said, "but I can brush my doll's hair with him.

And I can clean my football boots with him.

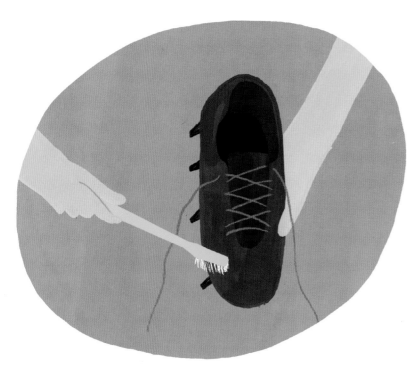

And paint with him.
He's still very useful."

Sammy now lives in a jam jar,
on a shelf in the toy cupboard.
When Sofia sleeps, the toys beg him
to tell them the story of how the
toothbrush travelled the world.

FROM AROUND THE WORLD

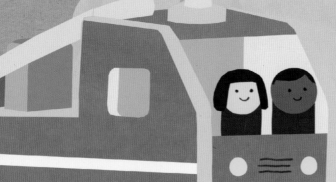

"I rode in a truck, sailed on a ship and got dragged by a rat. I floated across the ocean with the stars for guidance. I flew back to Sofia in the beak of an albatross, because, without a use and someone to love us, we are all rubbish."

THE PROBLEM

Many toothbrushes can't be recycled because they are made of a mix of plastics that are difficult to separate.

Nearly all the toothbrushes in the world are made from plastic. Their bodies are plastic and their bristles are made of nylon fibres.

plastic

nylon fibres

But you only use a toothbrush for three or four months. That's more than three toothbrushes every year. During your life you will use roughly three hundred toothbrushes.

When we throw plastic away, some is recycled, but most of it is buried, burned or ends up in our oceans.

WITH PLASTIC

A toothbrush is only one kind of plastic item we create.
How many other types can you spot in this story?

On average, eight million pieces of plastic enter our oceans every single day. This is very bad for the sea creatures who live there.

Plastic has been found washed up on beaches all around the world.

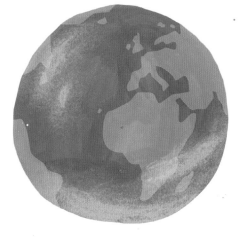

Why don't you try using a bamboo toothbrush?

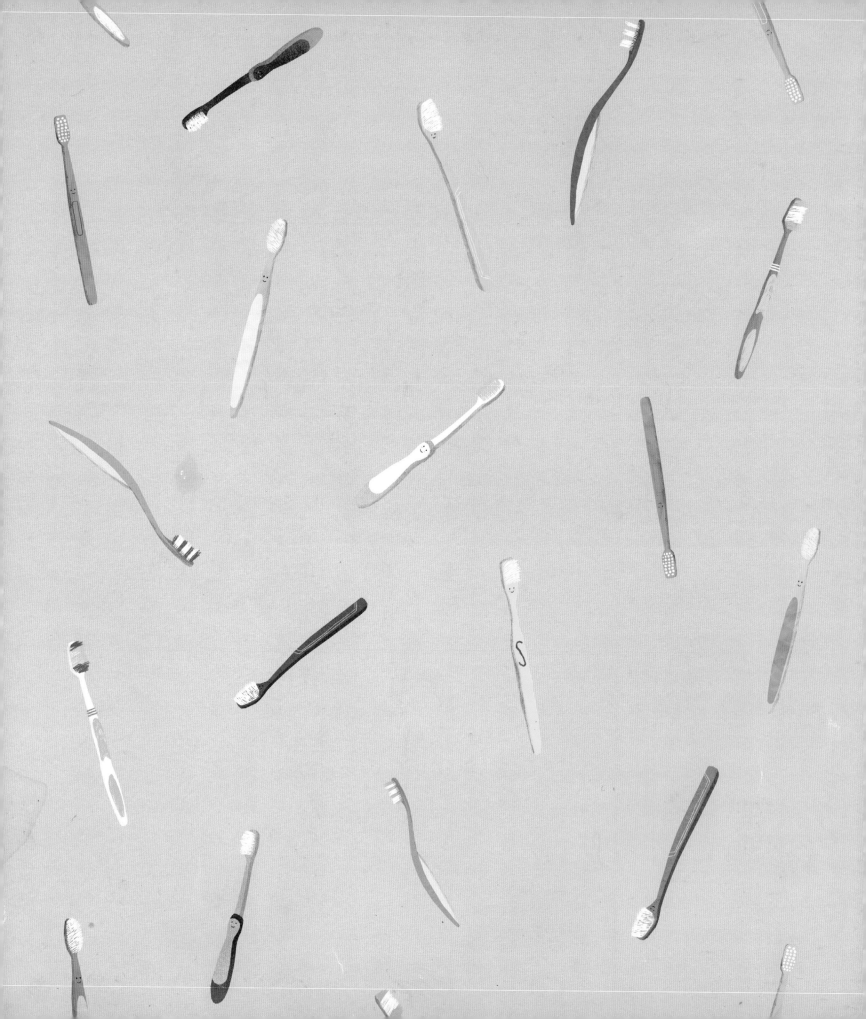